Morag The Tickling Midgie

By A.K. Paterson

LOMOND

First Published in Great Britain in 2008
Lomond Books Ltd
14 Freskyn Place, Broxburn, EH52 5NF
www.lomondbooks.com
ISBN 978-1-84204-085-0
Printed in China

It is the start of the school holidays. The Bell family have packed their tent and all the things they need for camping. Mr and Mrs Bell and their children, Billy and Heather, head for Bridge-of-Midge.
Bridge-of-Midge is a little village in the Highlands of Scotland.

On the edge of Bridge-of-Midge live Morag MacMidge and her family - Mum and Dad, Mary and Moray MacMidge, and her brother, Jock.

The MacMidges are preparing for their busiest time of the year - the Scottish Summer. Moray and Jock get ready to greet the visitors with stings and bites. Mary and Morag are also preparing for the tourist invasion. Morag's mother belongs to a rare clan of midgies - The Tickling Midgie. Long ago, Mary's ancestors threw away their stings, stopped biting and took up tickling instead!

The Bells have pitched their tent at the edge of Loch Ochaye.
They are looking forward to a happy week in the Highlands......

However, there is a storm on the horizon!

The Bells usually go to Spain on holiday. This year they decided to stay in Scotland. As well as all the camping stuff, they have packed all sorts of things to keep away the biting and stinging midgies!

Morag and Jock decide to pay a visit to Heather and Billy.
Unfortunately for Billy, Jock MacMidge has decided not to follow the tickling
ways of his Mum's family!

As the summer goes on, more and more visitors arrive in Bridge-of-Midge.
The MacMidge family are busier than ever!

A few days later and the Scottish Summer is over!

This is the time when the MacMidge family go on their winter holiday to Florida. Every year they visit their American cousins, the Mozzies!

Marvin and Mimi
Mozzie and their kids,
Melvin and Mo, get
ready for the arrival of
their Scottish cousins.

Morag and Jock are always very excited about visiting their American cousins. It makes a change from Bridge-of-Midge!

On a visit to Waterworld, Morag sees her old friend Heather Bell! Heather and Billy are also on holiday, visiting their cousins. Morag wants to go and say 'Hello!'. She takes Jock with her.

Maybe Morag's idea wasn't such a good one after all!

Their holidays over, the Bells and the MacMidges return home to Scotland.

A few weeks later, in a big castle, in the far North, The Queen of The Midgies has come back from a long visit to London.

The Queen is looking in on what her subjects have been up to. Suddenly she sees Morag doing something that she thought had died out many years ago!

The Queen gathers her staff and sets out for Bridge-of-Midge.
She decides not to fly because it makes her ears pop!

The Queen tells Morag that she, too, comes from an old family of Tickling Midgies!
However, when she married, she had to give up tickling and take up the stinging ways of her husband.
Now she feels the time is right for a return to tickling! And in Morag, she has found the right midgie to get the other midgies to take up the call to tickle!

Morag teaches her friends how to stop biting and stinging.

Midgies have been stinging for so long that they need a lot of help in learning how to tickle!

Morag decides to go and speak to the most powerful midgies in Scotland!

She tries to make the Midgie Parliament pass a law which will ban biting and stop stinging!

The MMPs - Members of the Midgie Parliament - vote to support Morag and tickling!

All stinging and biting is banned across the land!

Morag MacMidge has managed to get everyone on her side. Almost everyone! There is still one person she needs to win over!

A few months later...
Now that the stinging ban is in place, the Bells head back for the Highlands.

Stinging and biting has been stamped out all over Scotland.
But Morag still has work to do to persuade others that tickling is the
way forward......!